The Magic School Bus
Inside a Hurricane

The Magic School Bus

Inside a Hurricane

By Joanna Cole

Illustrated by Bruce Degen

Scholastic Inc.

New York · Toronto · London · Auckland · Sydney

The author and illustrator wish to thank Dr. Robert C. Sheets,
Director of the National Hurricane Center, and Dr. Daniel Leathers,
Delaware State Climatologist, University of Delaware,
for their assistance in preparing this book.

ISBN 0-590-44687-8
Text copyright © 1995 by Joanna Cole
Illustrations copyright © 1995 by Bruce Degen
Cover illustration © 1997 by Bruce Degen
Published by Scholastic Inc.

12   13   14   15   16   17   18   19   20   05   04   03   02

Printed in the U.S.A.   37
Revised format

The illustrator used pen and ink, watercolor,
color pencil, and gouache for the paintings in this book.

She's the Magic School Bus Editor
And we'd like herewith to credit her:
To Phoebe Yeh
Our Sunny Day.

J.C. & B.D.

We were learning about weather.
Absolutely everything in our room
was about rain or snow or sun or wind.
Every kid in the class
was doing a weather project.
We were even listening to
weather reports on Ms. Frizzle's radio.

TODAY'S MATH

SPELLING WORDS

Sun	Wind
rain	snow
drizzle	sleet
hail	hurricane
don't	forget
your	umbrella

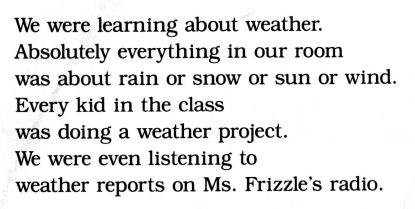

AT MY OLD SCHOOL WE DIDN'T HAVE ALL THESE PROJECTS!

AT MY OLD SCHOOL OUR TEACHER DIDN'T DRESS THAT WAY.

ANEMOMETER measures wind, force and speed.

AND NOW FOR THE WEATHER...

Our Snowflakes by Michael and Keesha

Wind Sock

WEATHER FORECASTING MADE EASY

WEATHERMAN

HAIL and HEARTY

RAIN

SNOW

ADVENTURES OF WEATHERMAN

WEATHERMAN FACES THE STORM

WEATHERMAN MEETS SNOWMAN

THE EARTH IS WRAPPED IN A BLANKET OF AIR
by Tim

EARTH — ATMOSPHERE

Our atmosphere is a blanket of air hundreds of miles thick.

Most of our weather happens in the troposphere — the 8 miles of air that is closest to earth.

THE ATMOSPHERE   MILES HIGH

68+ Thermosphere
50 Mesosphere
30 Stratosphere
8 Troposphere
0 EARTH

MOST WEATHER HAPPENS HERE.

So we weren't surprised one morning when Ms. Frizzle said, "It's a perfect day for our trip to the weather station!"

WE'LL MEET A TEAM OF WEATHER FORECASTERS. WE'LL LEARN ABOUT OUR ATMOSPHERE!

MS. FRIZZLE SAYS WE HAVE TO KNOW ABOUT AIR TO UNDERSTAND WEATHER.

AND WE HAVE TO KNOW ABOUT WATER, TOO.

I CAN'T SEE IT.

AIR

AIR IS A MIXTURE OF INVISIBLE GASES.
by Shirley

AIR HAS WEIGHT.
by Ralphie

A balloon with air in it is heavier than an empty balloon.

AIR CONTAINS WATER
by Wanda

1 DAY   2 DAYS   3 DAYS

When water evaporates, water molecules go into the air.

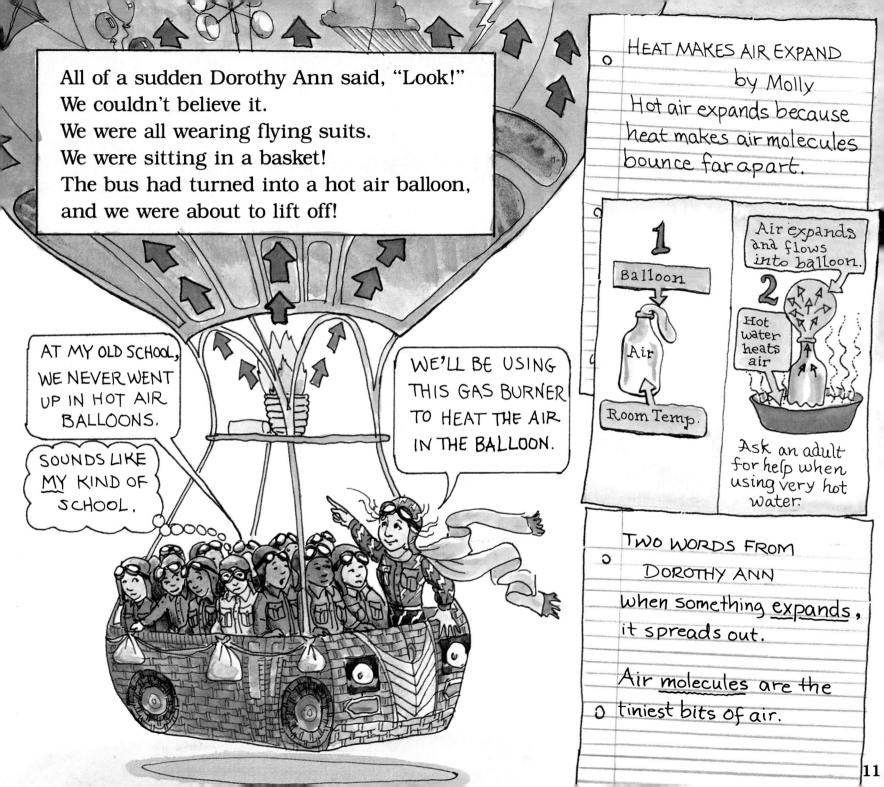

All of a sudden Dorothy Ann said, "Look!"
We couldn't believe it.
We were all wearing flying suits.
We were sitting in a basket!
The bus had turned into a hot air balloon,
and we were about to lift off!

AT MY OLD SCHOOL, WE NEVER WENT UP IN HOT AIR BALLOONS.

SOUNDS LIKE MY KIND OF SCHOOL.

WE'LL BE USING THIS GAS BURNER TO HEAT THE AIR IN THE BALLOON.

HEAT MAKES AIR EXPAND
by Molly
Hot air expands because heat makes air molecules bounce far apart.

1
Balloon
Air
Room Temp.

Air expands and flows into balloon.
2
Hot water heats air

Ask an adult for help when using very hot water.

TWO WORDS FROM DOROTHY ANN
when something expands, it spreads out.

Air molecules are the tiniest bits of air.

11

We rose higher and higher.
Even though hot air was filling the balloon,
the air around us was growing colder.
We had to put on warm jackets.

GOING UP?
BETTER BUNDLE UP!
by Phoebe

BRRR.

Warm air rises
from earth.
As it goes up,
it gets colder.

IT'S COLD UP HERE!

YOU'RE NOT AFRAID
OF HIGH PLACES,
ARE YOU, ARNOLD?

THAT RADIO SPOKE TO ME!

HOW DID IT KNOW MY
NAME?

I KNEW I SHOULD HAVE
STAYED HOME TODAY.

YOU CAN'T SEE IT,
BUT IT'S ALL
AROUND YOU.
WHAT IS IT?

Riddle
Book

AIR!

A WEATHER WORD
         by Dorothy Ann
When water <u>condenses</u>,
molecules of water vapor
join together and make
drops of liquid water.

"Warm air rising from earth carries lots of water vapor molecules," Ms. Frizzle continued. "As the air rises, it cools down. The water condenses in the air and forms clouds."

DID YOU BRING YOUR RAINCOAT, ARNOLD?

TELL ME THIS ISN'T HAPPENING....

We drifted into the center of a cloud.
Ms. Frizzle was right — it was *damp* in there.
The cloud was made of tiny water droplets
hanging in the air.

Down below, the weather forecasters were standing in the rain.
They didn't see us inside the cloud, but we could hear their voices.
One of them said, "I hope that teacher knows there's a *hurricane watch* in effect."

CHECK OUT MY HURRICANE WATCH, ARNOLD. GET IT? HURRICANE WATCH!!

I'M PRETENDING I CAN'T HEAR....

WHAT IS A HURRICANE?
by Florrie
A hurricane is one of the most violent kinds of storms.
In a hurricane, winds swirl in a circle around the storm's center at 74 miles per hour or more!

HURRICANE SYMBOL

MORE WORDS FROM DOROTHY ANN
A Hurricane <u>Watch</u> means that a hurricane may strike within the next 36 hours.
A Hurricane <u>Warning</u> means that a hurricane is likely to strike within the next 24 hours.
A warning is more urgent than a <u>watch</u>.

17

WHAT IS THE EQUATOR?
by Carlos

The equator is an imaginary line around the earth's middle. It divides the globe into two equal parts.

EQUATOR

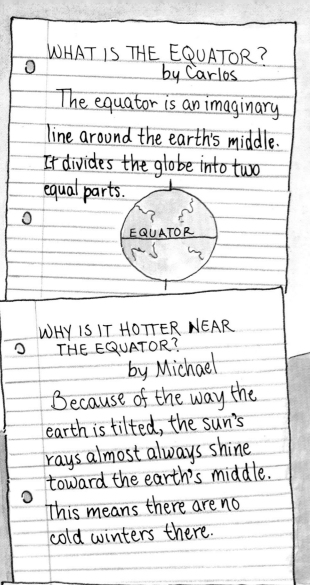

WHY IS IT HOTTER NEAR THE EQUATOR?
by Michael

Because of the way the earth is tilted, the sun's rays almost always shine toward the earth's middle. This means there are no cold winters there.

SUN

MOST DIRECT RAYS

NORTH POLE

EQUATOR

SOUTH POLE

THE TROPICS

As usual, Ms. Frizzle paid no attention.
She turned up the fire, and more
hot air rushed into the balloon.
As we rose above the cloud,
the wind started pushing us south.
Before long, we had traveled thousands of miles.
Ms. Frizzle said we were above a tropical ocean
about five hundred miles north of the equator.

WOW! LOOK AT THAT WATER!

WE CAN GO SWIMMING!

AND WINDSURFING!

AND SNORKELING!

Below us, blue-green waves were sparkling.
On a sandy island, palm trees were waving.
It looked like a vacation paradise to us.
But Frizzie said, "Class, we have now arrived
at one of the world's hurricane breeding grounds!"

NEARLY ALL HURRICANES GET STARTED OVER WARM TROPICAL OCEANS, KIDS.

I'VE HEARD THAT HURRICANES ARE DANGEROUS.

SO MS. FRIZZLE IS TAKING US TO ONE.

SHE WOULD!

WHY DO HURRICANES HAVE NAMES?
by Carmen

Often, more than one hurricane is brewing at once. It's easier to keep track of them if they are given names.

Some famous hurricanes:

- Agnes
- Andrew
- Bob
- Elena
- Gilbert
- Gloria
- Hugo

HI BOB!

WHAT'S HAPPENING GLORIA?

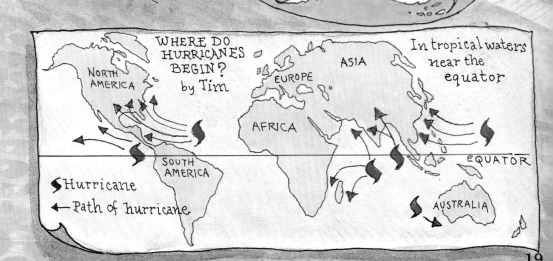

WHERE DO HURRICANES BEGIN?
by Tim

In tropical waters near the equator

NORTH AMERICA
SOUTH AMERICA
EUROPE
ASIA
AFRICA
AUSTRALIA
EQUATOR

$ Hurricane
← Path of hurricane

WHEN IS HURRICANE SEASON?
by Rachel

Most hurricanes begin in the late summer and early fall. That is when tropical oceans are warmest.

The warmer the ocean is, the stronger the hurricane is likely to become.

"Class, remember that as hot air rises from the ocean surface, the water vapor in the air condenses and forms clouds," said the Friz.
Down below, more hot air rushed in from all sides to take the place of the rising air.
In the middle of the rising air,
a column of sinking air formed.
We started sinking with it.

WATER VAPOR CONDENSES

AIR COOLS THEN SINKS

WARM, MOIST AIR RISES

A HURRICANE IS STARTING!

OUR BALLOON IS FALLING!

OH, NO!

SINKING AIR

WINDS

WINDS

RAIN

RAIN

WARM, MOIST AIR BLOWS

WARM OCEAN SURFACE

"Oh dear," said Ms. Frizzle.
"The balloon must have sprung a leak."
Hot air was rushing out, and the balloon
was plummeting fast.
"Jump ship, class!" shouted the Friz.
She jumped overboard, and we went after her.
Right away, we knew it was a big mistake.

HURRY UP AND
JUMP, ARNOLD!

I CAN'T LOOK!

FOLLOW
ME, KIDS!

21

WHAT MAKES HURRICANE WINDS BLOW IN A CIRCLE?
by Alex

Winds begin by blowing straight. But the movement of the earth as it spins on its axis makes them curve.

WINDS CURVE

THE EARTH SPINS →

AXIS

The faster winds blow, the more they curve. Hurricane winds are <u>very</u> fast, so they curve and curve until they make a circle.

The wind was blowing the clouds into a huge circle.
"The storm is starting to take on the typical shape of a hurricane. Isn't it fascinating, children?" shouted Ms. Frizzle.

HELP!

WE'RE GOING AROUND IN CIRCLES!

I'M GETTING DIZZY!

It was more than fascinating.
It was terrifying!
We were caught in the edge of the storm,
blowing around and around in a giant whirlwind.
That whirlwind was a hurricane!

HOW BIG IS A HURRICANE?
by John
Hurricanes are enormous. Each one is about 10 miles high and 300 to 600 miles wide!

A TYPICAL HURRICANE HAS A LIFE SPAN OF ABOUT 10 DAYS.

LISTENERS— WE'LL BE TELLING YOU ABOUT THE WHOLE HURRICANE.

MAYBE ITS BATTERIES WILL RUN OUT SOON.

Where We Are in the Hurricane

All around were columns of air
called hot towers, or chimneys.
They were sucking up more and more
hot moist air from the ocean.
The heat energy from the air
was feeding the storm
and making it stronger.
The plane was shaking
and so were we!

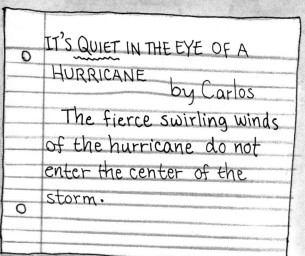

IT'S QUIET IN THE EYE OF A HURRICANE
by Carlos

The fierce swirling winds of the hurricane do not enter the center of the storm.

Land
Arnold
Eye wall
Eye
Where we are in the Hurricane

Then suddenly everything was quiet.
"Class, we have entered the eye — or center —
of the hurricane!" announced Ms. Frizzle.
The ocean waves still crashed below
and the winds howled outside,
but in the eye only gentle breezes blew.
Up above, the sky was blue
and the sun was shining.
We relaxed and enjoyed ourselves.

We flew about thirty miles
across the eye.
Then the Friz called out,
"We will enter the other side
of the eye wall now."
"Don't go!" we cried,
but the plane was already
on its way — back into the
hurricane's fierce wind and rain.

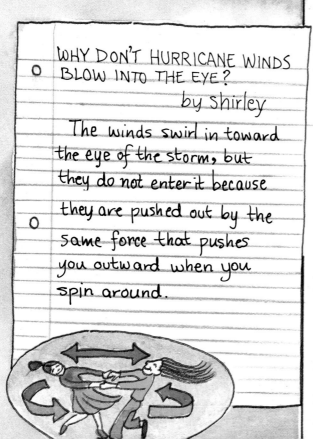

WHY DON'T HURRICANE WINDS BLOW INTO THE EYE?
by Shirley

The winds swirl in toward the eye of the storm, but they do not enter it because they are pushed out by the same force that pushes you outward when you spin around.

HOW HURRICANES TRAVEL
by Wanda

When a hurricane starts, it usually moves slowly—about 10 to 20 miles per hour. As the storm gets farther north, its speed can increase up to 60 miles per hour! Hurricanes can travel hundreds of miles each day.

WHICH PART OF THE HURRICANE IS STRONGEST?
by Florrie

The right front corner is strongest because the whirling winds are circling toward the shore. They add their strength to the winds that move the storm forward.

The entire hurricane was moving across the ocean toward land, and we were going with it! "The right forward corner of the hurricane as you are looking toward land has the strongest wind and rain and the highest ocean waves," shouted the Friz. Naturally, she flew directly into that part.

But that was nothing compared to the horror we felt when we heard the Friz shouting above the sound of roaring water,
"We seem to be running out of gas, children!"
Sure enough, the plane was dipping lower and lower.

As we fell into the water, we saw Arnold waving to us from a nearby roof.

Somehow Arnold managed to get on the plane
before we were swept away by the waves
at the front edge of the hurricane.
The water was creeping up the windows.
The plane was going to sink for sure!
Then we saw a dark, funnel shape coming our way.

"I've seen that shape on TV," said Ralphie.
"I read about it in a book!" said Keesha.
The twister came right for us.
The next thing we knew, it had picked us up,
and we were traveling by tornado!

TORNADOES OFTEN OCCUR AT THE EDGES OF HURRICANES THAT ARE MOVING OVER LAND, CLASS.

ARE TORNADOES AND HURRICANES ALIKE?
by Phil

Yes and no.
Tornadoes and hurricanes are both whirlwinds.
But tornadoes:
1. are much smaller than hurricanes
2. have faster winds, for the most part
3. destroy almost everything in their path.

Tornadoes can twist at speeds of 200 to 300 miles per hour.

A TYPICAL TORNADO HAS A SHORT LIFE SPAN— ONLY A FEW MINUTES.

I THINK MY LIFE SPAN JUST GOT SHORTER.

CAN TORNADOES REALLY CARRY OBJECTS?
by Keesha

Yes! Tornadoes are like giant vacuum cleaners. They lift dirt, trash, and even large objects, such as houses, cars, trees, and railroad trains!

Once a tornado picked up a crate of eggs and set them down miles away. Not one egg was broken!

After a while we felt a bump and looked around.
The tornado had set us down gently.
We were in our old school bus again.
We were dressed in our regular clothes again.
The hurricane was over.
And we were at a gas station.

USUALLY THE THINGS THAT ARE PICKED UP BY A TORNADO ARE BROKEN APART...

BUT NOT ALWAYS.

THANK GOODNESS!

CLUCK CLUCK EGGS   No CRACKS No QUACKS

REGULAR   SUPER   MAGIC

Ms. Frizzle filled up the tank
and drove down the road
as if nothing had happened.
"As I said earlier, class, we are on our way
to visit a weather station," she said.

TAKE OUR CASE, FOR EXAMPLE. WE'RE ALL OKAY.

EVEN THE RADIO IS STILL WORKING FINE.

HERE'S A TREAT JUST FOR YOU, ARNOLD—ANOTHER WEATHER UPDATE....

THAT DEPENDS ON WHAT YOU MEAN BY "WORKING FINE."

GAS

After that trip, we needed some time to relax.
Ms. Frizzle said we could have a party.
We had great games, crazy dancing, and yummy snacks.
And for a while, we didn't even think about
Ms. Frizzle's next class trip!

The Magic School Bus Mail Bag
Letters... we get letters...

To the Magic School Bus Editor: You should not have said that a school bus could turn into a hot air balloon or a weather plane. That cannot really happen. Your friend, Sam

EXOTIC BROOKLYN

FOR SALE

Dear Joanna, Radios cannot have conversations with people. Barbara

TO: JOANNA COLE AUTHOR c/o Scholastic Inc.

GREETINGS FROM SUNNY EAST ORANGE, N.J.

Dear Joanna and Bruce, Reading about hurricanes may be fun, but it is no fun to be in one! I know because my family was in Hurricane ANDREW and it was scary! — Keith

Dear Bruce, Radios do not dance. from Jean

TO: Bruce Degen ARTIST c/o Scholastic Inc.

Dear Arnold, On your trip, the hurricane reached land. But most hurricanes go far out to sea and do not hurt people and property. Your friend, Al, the weather scientist

A fishing boat probably would not survive if it were out in a very strong hurricane. From the Coast Guard